3.00

Words to Know Before You Read

already

bites

broccoli

everything

perfectly

really

www.rourkepublishing.com

Edited by Luana Mitten
Illustrated by Anita DuFalla
Art Direction and Page Layout by Renee Brady

Library of Congress Cataloging-in-Publication Data

Robertson, J. Jean
 How Many Bites? / J. Jean Robertson.
    p. cm. -- (Little Birdie Books)
 ISBN 978-1-61741-801-3 (hard cover) (alk. paper)
 ISBN 978-1-61236-005-8 (soft cover)
 Library of Congress Control Number: 2011924653

Rourke Publishing
Printed in the United States of America, North Mankato, Minnesota
060711
060711CL

www.rourkepublishing.com - rourke@rourkepublishing.com
Post Office Box 643328 Vero Beach, Florida 32964

HOW MANY BITES?

By J. Jean Robertson

Illustrated by Anita DuFalla

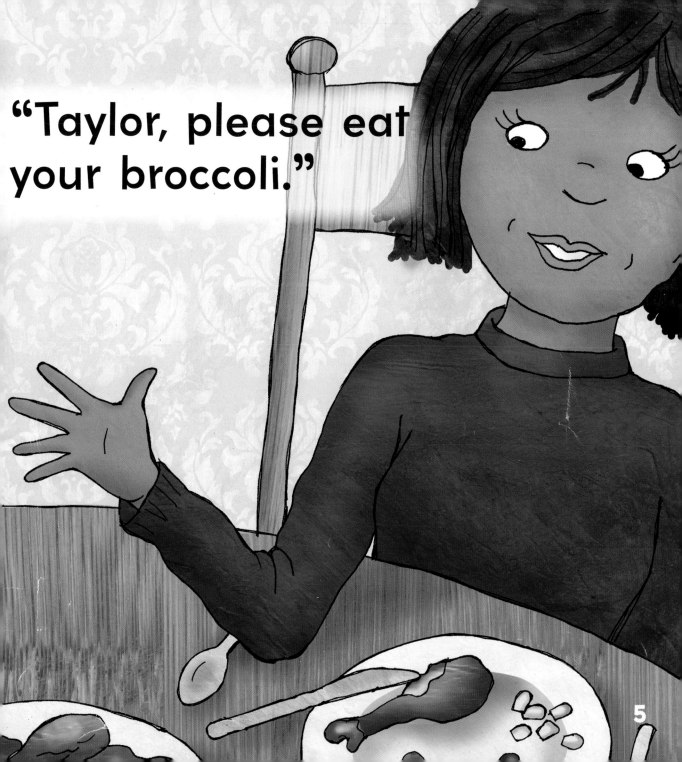

"Mom, I'm already full."

8

"But Mom, why do I need broccoli?"

"Broccoli is a perfectly good food."

13

"Broccoli does not look good to me."

"Fine. Close your eyes
while you eat it."

"You know we try some of everything."

"OK. How many bites?"

After Reading Activities

You and the Story...

What food didn't Taylor want to try?

What food do you dislike?

What is your favorite food?

Tell a friend about the foods you like and foods you dislike.

Words You Know Now...

Can you write a sentence that uses all of the words listed below?
Share your sentence with a friend.

already	everything
bites	perfectly
broccoli	really

You Could...Cook Dinner with Your Family

- Look at a cookbook to decide what you would like to fix for dinner.

- Plan the menu with your family. Don't forget to consider what everyone likes to eat.

- Make sure your menu has a main course, side dishes, and dessert.

- Make a list of all the ingredients needed for each item on the menu.
    - Check to see what you already have in your kitchen.
    - Make a grocery list of things you need to buy for your dinner.

- Go shopping for your grocery items.

- Decide who is going to make each dish and start cooking.

- YUM! Enjoy your dinner!

About the Author

J. Jean Robertson, also known as Bushka to her grandchildren and many other kids, lives in San Antonio, Florida with her husband. She is retired after many years of teaching. She loves to read, travel, and write books for children AND she also loves to eat vegetables, especially broccoli!

About the Illustrator

Acclaimed for its versatility in style, Anita DuFalla's work has appeared in many educational books, newspaper articles, and business advertisements and on numerous posters, book and magazine covers, and even giftwraps. Anita's passion for pattern is evident in both her artwork and her collection of 400 patterned tights. She lives in the Friendship neighborhood of Pittsburgh, Pennsylvania with her son, Lucas.